The EAGLE STORY

How to Conquer Habits

This Book Belongs
to

INSTITUTE IN BASIC YOUTH CONFLICTS, INC.
Box One Oak Brook, Illinois 60522-3001

Printed in the United States of America.

Sixth Printing, June 1987

ISBN 0-916888-07-X

Library of Congress
Catalog Card Number: 81-85536

Meet The MONARCH of THE SKY

PART ONE

THE WAYS OF THE EAGLE

SIGNIFICANT FEATURES EMPHASIZED BY GOD IN THE BIBLE

- The Swiftness of the Eagle

- The Power of the Eagle's Wings

- The Wonder of an Eagle in the Air

- The Sudden Attack of the Eagle

- The Height of the Eagles' Nest

- The Eagles' Care of Their Young

- The Sharp Eyes of an Eagle

- The Soaring Heights of an Eagle

- The Eagle as a Symbol

How Well Do You Know the Eagle?

WHAT GOD REVEALS ABOUT THE EAGLE

THE SWIFTNESS OF THE EAGLE[1]

1. How swiftly does the eagle fly?

A great bald eagle was once observed flying across a lake in less than one minute. The lake was two miles wide; thus the average speed of the eagle was calculated to be 120 miles per hour. This meant that speeds in excess of 150 miles per hour had been achieved during the flight.

When searching for prey, the eagle can soar to a height of one-half mile. From that vantage point the eagle can survey an area of some four and one-half square miles. Upon spotting its intended prey, the eagle will turn sharply, fold its wings into a tight, aerodynamic formation, and dive at speeds of up to 200 miles per hour!

2. Why do eagles appear to be slow?

The soaring eagle may appear to be lazy and sluggish to the casual observer. However, if the observer is aware of the eagle's large size and the great heights to which it soars, he will not be so easily deceived. The eagle's seven-foot wingspan allows it to glide effortlessly at altitudes of over 2,400 feet, thus giving the illusion that the eagle is moving at a "snail's pace."

THE POWER OF THE EAGLE'S WINGS[2]

1. How powerful are the eagle's wings?

The eagle is capable of carrying objects which approach its own body weight. Since an eagle can weigh up to twelve pounds, the variety of what it can carry is tremendous. Eagles have been known to transport small lambs a distance of several miles.

1. See II Samuel 1:23; Deuteronomy 28:49.
2. See Ezekiel 17:3; Jeremiah 49:22; Isaiah 40:31.

THE WONDER OF AN EAGLE IN THE AIR[1]

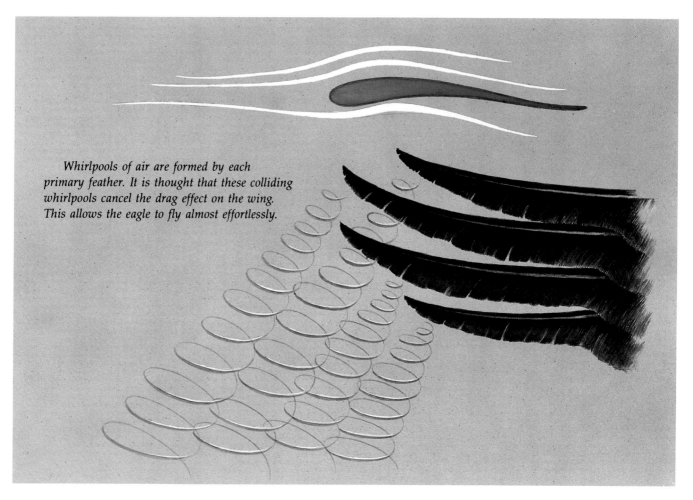

Whirlpools of air are formed by each primary feather. It is thought that these colliding whirlpools cancel the drag effect on the wing. This allows the eagle to fly almost effortlessly.

1. What are the "secrets" of the eagle's wings?

The eagle's wings are characterized by primary feathers which are separated at the tips like the fingers of a hand. These separations play a major role in the power and stability of the eagle in flight. Air passes more quickly over the tops of the wings than the bottoms, thus creating lift. The difference between the two air speeds also causes spinning whirls of air to form near the wing tips, creating "drag" which would normally slow the eagle down. However, because the primary feathers are separated, many small whirlpools are formed instead of one large one. Scientists propose that as the spinning currents expand, they collide and cancel the drag effect, thus enabling the eagle to fly almost indefinitely.

Eagles flap their wings mainly at takeoff and during acceleration when pursuing prey. While soaring, the eagle uses the movement of the wing tips and the furling of the wings to achieve sustained flight.

2. Can an eagle fly in a hurricane?

The same separation of the primary feathers which reduces drag also serves to provide greater stability in flight. The eagle folds its wings slightly toward its body, thus reducing the total wing capacity. Eagles have been seen soaring almost motionlessly in near hurricane-force winds, moving only the tips of their primary feathers to adjust for the varying wind speeds.

3. How many feathers does an eagle have?

One eagle was found to have 7,182 feathers. Each wing had over 1,250 feathers, which accounted for sixteen percent of the bird's total body weight.

1. See Proverbs 30:18–19.

4. How is the eagle "renewed" each year?

Each year the eagle replaces its feathers over a period of several months. However, unlike other birds, the eagle is not severely handicapped during this time, because no two adjacent wing feathers fall out, or moult, at the same time. Thus, the eagle is able to continue hunting throughout the entire renewal process.

THE SUDDEN ATTACK OF THE EAGLE[1]

1. What do eagles hunt?

The eagle is an efficient hunter, killing only what is necessary for food. Eagles seek carrion (dead flesh), fresh fish, water fowl, and small land animals such as squirrels, chickens, foxes, and raccoons.

2. Does an eagle steal food?

Yes. For example, an eagle may patiently wait perched in the top of a tree while an osprey hunts for fish. As the osprey dips into the water and begins to fly away with a prize fish, the eagle swoops into action, harrassing the osprey until it drops the fish. The eagle will then dive at great speed to snatch the prize for itself before it hits the water!

3. How does an eagle attack upside down?

The eagle attacks from a perch or soaring position high above its prey. With incredible speed the eagle usually overcomes its victim with complete surprise. One of the most spectacular displays is the attack on a water fowl in flight. Swooping down from behind, the eagle attacks from underneath by rolling over onto its back and thrusting its talons into the breast of the victim. Both begin to tumble toward the water below. With smaller birds, the eagle may recover in midair. With larger ones, such as the Canadian goose, both eagle and prey hit the water together. The eagle then tows its victim to shore.

1. See Habakkuk 1:8; Lamentations 4:19; Jeremiah 4:13; Job 9:26.

THE HEIGHT OF THE EAGLES' NEST[1]

1. Why do eagles build such high nests?

Eagles' nests are typically built as high as possible. Golden eagles seek the highest recesses of mountain cliffs, while bald eagles nest in the tops of the tallest trees. The height serves three purposes: a protection for the young, a perch for surveying the territory, and an energy-saving launching pad for the adult eagle. As it swoops down from its nest, the eagle is able to gain sufficient speed for its gradual climb into the sky.

2. How do eagles fell trees?

Eagles mate for life and return to the same nest each year, making necessary repairs and additions. One pair of eagles was observed for thirty-five years in the same location. Their nest grew to be twenty feet deep and nine and one-half feet across! Because of the ever-increasing weight of such nests, support trees often give way, and the nesting eagles are forced to start anew.

3. How do eagles decorate their nests?

After the nest is remodeled and made ready for the eggs, the eagles decorate the nest with a sprig of greenery. Most often a branch from a white pine is chosen, although each pair of eagles apparently have their own preference.

1. See Jeremiah 49:16; Ezekiel 17:3–4.

THE EAGLES' CARE OF THEIR YOUNG[1]

1. How is the sun the eagle's enemy?

Because eagles seek the highest points upon which to build their nests, there is no shade to protect their young from the sun's intense heat. Therefore, when a parent eagle leaves the nest, it replaces its body's shade with a layer of sticks and debris. The eagle will often spend five to ten minutes with this procedure, making sure the young are adequately protected.

2. Why do eaglets compete with each other?

The "brood" may contain two or three eaglets. The first eaglet to hatch is usually the largest and demands the most food, causing keen competition among the young eaglets. During the first few weeks, the nestlings are fed by the mother eagle. The father eagle does the hunting and delivers the meal to the mother, who then rips the prey into bite-size portions. The parent eagles continue to supply food for the eaglets throughout the summer months, until the youngsters have developed adequate flying and hunting skills.

3. How do eagles teach their young to fly?

After spending two or three months in the security of the nest, the young eagle is ready to fly. The first flight is usually to a nearby branch or rock. On subsequent flights the adult eagle may accompany the eaglet, using its primary feathers to create an air current which actually lifts the eaglet. During the period of flight training, parent eagles will often coax their young eaglets to fly by perching on nearby trees or rocks with food and then calling the youngsters to come.

4. How do eagles "bare" their young on their wings?

In Exodus 19:4, God states "... I bare you on eagle's wings. ..." The Hebrew word, bare is nâçâh. Its primary root means "to lift." This is precisely what the eagle does with the wind currents from its wing tips.

1. See Exodus 19:4; Deuteronomy 32:11.

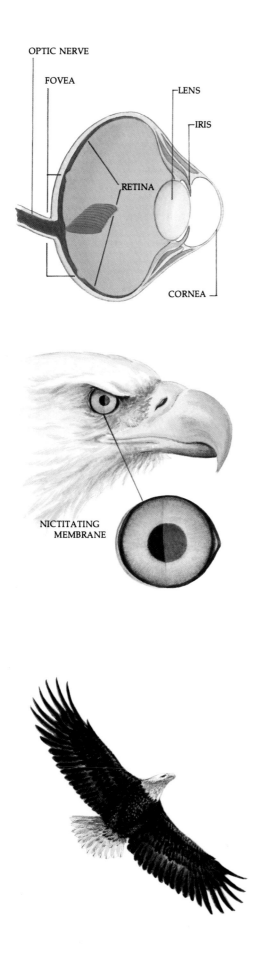

NICTITATING
MEMBRANE

THE SHARP EYES OF AN EAGLE

1. How does the eagle have double vision?

The eagle's vision is exceptionally sharp because each eye has two "fovea" (areas of acute vision), as compared with the human eye, which has only one. The "cones" in the eagle's fovea are very small and tightly grouped, allowing the eagle to see small details from extreme distances. For example, an eagle can spot an object as small as a rabbit from a distance of almost two miles! A man, however, would have to look through a pair of powerful binoculars to see the same thing.

The eyes are placed forward on the eagle's head, giving it accurate depth perception. This is important because when an eagle is pursuing its prey, it must know precisely when to pull out of a dive. The forward placement of its eyes also enables the eagle to see to each side (peripheral vision). The eagle's area of vision covers almost 270 degrees—much more than man's.

2. How can the eagle see with its eyes "shut"?

In addition to its normal pair of eyelids, the eagle has a set of clear eyelids called "nictitating membranes." These eyelids can be closed for protection from the wind, hungry eaglets, or the violence of the kill without affecting the eagle's vision.

THE SOARING HEIGHTS OF AN EAGLE

1. Why does God compare riches to an eagle?

In Proverbs 23:5, God warns us not to concentrate on becoming rich because "... *riches certainly make themselves wings; they fly away as an eagle toward heaven.*"

This illustration is a vivid one indeed. As it flies away, the eagle's size decreases in the eyes of the viewer until it is out of sight. When people become greedy, inflation results and the "size" of the dollar decreases until it has little or no value.

THE EAGLE AS A SYMBOL[1]

1. Why is the eagle chosen as a symbol?

The eagle has been revered and esteemed for thousands of years. No doubt one reason for this is the eagle's grandeur and grace in flight. Another reason is that with its head sitting regally between the shoulders formed by its folded wings, the eagle strikes a very "royal" pose. The eagle has also been admired for its great size and awesome power.

The eagle was the official symbol of the Romans, Charlemagne, and Napoleon; and today it is the dominant figure on the official seal of the United States.

2. How does the eagle display decisiveness?

The eagle is given its decisive look primarily by the structure of its eyes. Just above each eye is a bony protrusion which extends over the eye much like a furrowed eyebrow. These protrusions lend to the eagle's face the human expression of decisiveness. If the eagle lacked these protrusions, it would appear to be passive.

3. What letter of the alphabet does the eagle represent?

The ancient Egyptians used a symbolic alphabet of pictures called hieroglyphics. The picture of the eagle was used extensively in that alphabet. As written language developed, the symbol of the eagle eventually became the letter *a*.

1. God uses the eagle extensively as a symbol in presenting Scriptural truths such as in Revelation 4:7.

PART TWO

THE WARNINGS OF THE EAGLE

THIS STORY PROVIDES GRAPHIC WARNINGS OF THE DANGERS WHICH SURROUND OUR LIVES

•The Eagle Story

•Can You Detect Ten Aspects of
 Danger in the Story of the Eagle?

Adapted from *The Kindred of the Wild* by Charles G. D. Roberts
(Boston: L. C. Page and Co., 1902), pp. 55-92.

16

A Great Bald Eagle sat in tranquil dignity on his lookout high above the valley basin. The last wisp of vapor had vanished, drunk up by the rising sun. The sharp eye of the Eagle had clear command of every district in his realm.

*S*oon he launched majestically from his perch and sailed down over the jagged pine trees and gleaming lakes to his favorite fishing spot.

When the Eagle arrived, he noticed a slight change. A large rock had been placed near the shore. Since it was something new, it was to be suspect of danger.

19

*H*e flew over it without stopping, and alighted on the top of a dead tree nearby. After a piercing scrutiny, he was convinced that the rock was a provision for his convenience.

$\mathcal{H}$e sailed down and perched upon it. Then he saw a large fish lying on the grass. He considered again.

If the fish had been near the water's edge, he would have understood. But up on the grass — that was an uncommon situation for a fish to get itself into!

*T*he wise Eagle now peered suspiciously into the neighboring bushes. He scanned every grassy area and cast a sweeping survey up and down the shores. Everything was as it should be.

*S*o he hopped down, clutched the fish in his sharp claws, and was about to fly away when he caught sight of another fish, and yet another. Plainly, the wilderness was caring for his needs in a most unexpected and lavish way.

But across the lake, the sharp eyes of a cunning trapper studied every move which the Eagle made. This trapper had been offered a large sum of money to capture an eagle alive. He was a crafty and experienced trapper, and he knew that this wise monarch of the sky would not be snared by any ordinary means.

On the following day the great Eagle returned. He found that the supply of fish had been miraculously renewed. This provision would lighten his labors and give him more time to sit upon his wind-swept perch and to view his domain.

At every visit to his fishing spot he perched on the rock and devoured at least one fish before carrying a meal to his nest. His surprise and curiosity as to the source of the supply had died out by the second day. Wild creatures quickly come to accept an obvious benefit, however extraordinary, as one of those provisions which unseen powers bestow without explanation.

By the time that the Eagle had come to this frame of mind, the silent trapper was ready for his next move. He made a large, strong hoop-net and, on a moonlit night, carefully dug the long handle into the ground at the water's edge. He put it on an angle so that the hoop was almost level, about four feet from the rock.

Having accomplished this, the clever trapper scattered fish upon the ground. Then he disappeared into the bleakness of the forest.

On the following morning the mighty Eagle sat on his lookout. His intense gaze swept the vast, shadowy basin. For fully half an hour he watched in regal stillness. Then he lifted off his perch and flew leisurely to his fishing spot.

As he drew near, he was puzzled and annoyed by the odd structure which had been erected above his rock during the night. He at once checked his flight and began soaring in great circles.

Higher and higher he flew, trying in vain to make out what that strange-looking object was. He could see, however, that the fish were there as usual. At length he satisfied himself that no hidden peril lurked in the nearby bushes.

He descended to the nearest tree top and spent a good half hour in motionless scrutiny. He little guessed that a solitary figure, equally motionless and far more patient, was watching his every move from a thicket across the lake.

*A*t the end of this long watch the Eagle decided that a closer
investigation was desirable. He flew down to the sandy shore
well away from the net. He found a fish which he devoured.
Then he found another. This he carried away to his nest. He
had not solved the mystery of the strange structure overhanging
his rock, but he had proved that it was not actually dangerous.

When the Eagle returned an hour later,
the net looked less strange to him. He even
perched on the sloping handle. The structure
seemed quite harmless.

He hopped down and looked with keen interest at the fish lying under the hoop beside the rock. He reached out with beak and claw, clutched one fish, and quickly hopped back. The Eagle repeated this cautious procedure at every visit throughout the day.

But, when he came again on the next day, the Eagle had grown once more utterly confident. He went under the net without haste or apprehension and perched unconcernedly on the stone in the midst of his banquet.

The next morning, about an hour before dawn, a ghostly birch canoe slipped up to shore about a hundred yards from the net. The trapper stepped out, lifted the canoe from the water, and hid it in the bushes. Then he proceeded to make some important changes in the arrangement of the net.

First he tied a strong cord to the rim of the hoop. Then he ran the cord down to the ground, under a shallow root, and into a nearby thicket. He pulled on the cord. The net bent down until it covered the rock. When he released the cord, the net rebounded to its former position.

After satisfying himself that all was in readiness, he baited his trap with the usual fish and then crept under the thicket. There he waited in perfect stillness through the chill hours of the breaking day.

At last there came the sound of mighty wings in the still air above him. The trapper watched as the Eagle landed on the sand next to the rock. This time there was no hesitation. The great bird, for all his wisdom, had been lured into accepting the structure as part of the established order.

He hopped right under the net, clutched a large fish, and perched on the stone to enjoy his meal.

At that moment the Eagle sensed the shadow of a movement in the thicket. His muscles tightened for that instantaneous spring into the safety of the air. But before he could move, the large net came down about him with a terrible swish!

An intense struggle ensued between the bird and the net — beating wings, tearing beak, clutching talons. But soon the mighty Eagle was helplessly entangled in the meshes of the unyielding trap.

CAN YOU DETECT TEN ASPECTS OF DANGER IN THE STORY OF THE EAGLE?

1. Hidden dangers usually have visible evidences.

The most deadly traps are usually hidden; however, there are often visible evidences of their presence. In the book of Proverbs we read of a simple young man who went to the house of an immoral woman. Although there were many warnings of danger, he disregarded all of them. He paid a high price for his willingness to be trapped. (See Proverbs 7:6–27.)

Things that are unfamiliar should be carefully evaluated before being accepted. The Apostle Paul told his listeners to test even his teachings against other Scripture. (See Acts 17:11.) Scripture warns us, *"Beloved, believe not every spirit, but try the spirits whether they are of God: because many false prophets are gone out into the world" (I John 4:1).*

2. The most dangerous enemies are unseen.

The eagle in the story trusted in what he saw with his eyes. He made the mistake of ignoring his instincts. God warns us that the enemy we must fear the most is the unseen enemy of our soul, who tempts us to stop fearing God. God is to be feared above all since He is able to destroy both body and soul in hell. *"And fear not them which kill the body, but are not able to kill the soul: but rather fear him which is able to destroy both soul and body in hell" (Matthew 10:28).*

A spiritually mature Christian realizes that he is engaged in a spiritual warfare with unseen but very real powers of evil. *"For we wrestle not against flesh and blood, but against principalities, against powers, against the rulers of the darkness of this world, against spiritual wickedness in high places" (Ephesians 6:12).*

3. Deadly traps will always appeal to basic needs.

The clever trapper knew that what the eagle needed and enjoyed the most was fish; so every day he baited the trap with big, beautiful fish. Satan knows that we need food, clothing, acceptance, security, and companionship. He will offer these as bait to lure us into his traps.

When Satan tempted Christ in the wilderness, he tempted him with basic needs. Christ detected Satan's first bait of food and rejected it. As a result, Christ was then spiritually alert to Satan's further temptations. (See Matthew 4:1–11.) When the testing was finished, He was fed by angels.

4. "Instinctive cautions" warn of hidden danger.

The eagle had built-in senses to detect danger. These instincts should have been aroused by the gradual construction of a trap, but the eagle chose to ignore them.

God has also given us inner alarms to warn us of danger. God reinforces these alarms with promptings of the Holy Spirit (see Romans 8:13–14), warning from the Bible (see II Timothy 3:16–17), and instructions from our parents (see Proverbs 6:20–22) and pastors (see Hebrews 13:17). Satan knows that if his bait is attractive enough, we may be willing to set aside all of these cautions.

5. Free provisions have hidden costs.

The basic tendencies of greed and laziness produce the eagerness to get something for nothing. However, the fact is that there is a price tag for everything.

Even the free gift of salvation was only made possible by the payment of the blood of the Lord Jesus Christ. (See I Peter 1:18–19.)

Satan is very skillful in displaying the pleasures of sin without revealing the final price tag of them. He deceives us into thinking that either there is no cost or that the cost is insignificant. In reality, the wages of sin is more sin. The final price tag is staggering.

"Be not deceived; God is not mocked: for whatsoever a man soweth, that shall he also reap" (Galatians 6:7).

6. Life is built upon a cause-and-effect sequence.

Every day the eagle saw fish lying near the structure that was to become a trap. He did not know how the fish or the trap happened to be there, and what apprehension he did have about the free fish soon disappeared. The eagle began to depend on the availability of these fish, and his instincts for danger became dulled.

God warns us that there are two root causes behind the circumstances which affect our lives: God or Satan. For this reason, we cannot take the things that come into our lives as mere coincidences or accidents. We must discern their source. If we ignore this truth, we will find ourselves reaping painful consequences. *"For he that soweth to his flesh shall of the flesh reap corruption; but he that soweth to the Spirit shall of the Spirit reap life everlasting" (Galatians 6:8).*

7. There are built-in dangers to a life of ease.

The eagle gained fresh food every day, but he lost his alertness to impending danger. He became dull and sluggish. This loss of alertness ultimately cost him his freedom.

God warns us that we are never to work for a life of ease. The rich man, who spent many years accumulating wealth and then told himself that he could live in ease, was called a fool by God. (See Luke 12:16–21.)

Our promised rest is not here, but in heaven. While we are on this earth, we are to labor; for the night is coming when no man can work. (See John 9:4.)

8. Deadly traps look harmless until they are sprung.

The eagle had grown accustomed to his surroundings. He had come to accept the presence of the trap and no longer viewed it with suspicion and apprehension. It became a part of his world.

Satan also knows that we do not comprehend the deadly destruction of his harmless-looking traps. He wants us to minimize the consequences of sin while magnifying its pleasures.

Once Satan's traps are sprung, however, there are temporal and eternal consequences, not just for the one caught in the trap but for generations to come. "*. . . For I the Lord thy God am a jealous God, visiting the iniquity of the fathers upon the children unto the third and fourth generation of them that hate me*" *(Exodus 20:5).*

9. Once they are sprung, traps close too swiftly for escape.

The eagle acted quickly once he finally sensed danger, but he was no match for the swiftness of the trap's destructive action.

It is our pride and false confidence that tells us that we can enjoy the pleasures of sin and not get caught in its consequences.

God asks, "*Can a man take fire in his bosom, and his clothes not be burned? Can one go upon hot coals, and his feet not be burned? So he that goeth in to his neighbour's wife; whosoever toucheth her shall not be innocent*" *(Proverbs 6:27–29).*

10. Traps result in captivity or death unless the victim is freed.

Once the trap was sprung on the eagle, he lost his freedom. No longer would he soar in the heights above, or come and go as he pleased. He was now under the control of his captor. Any effort to free himself only resulted in greater destruction and bondage.

God warns us that if we yield our members to the lusts of the flesh, we will become the slaves of sin. "*Know ye not, that to whom ye yield yourselves servants to obey, his servants ye are to whom ye obey; whether of sin unto death, or of obedience unto righteousness?*" *(Romans 6:16).*

We can thank God, however, that there is a way to freedom from the bondage of sin. It is explained in the following pages.

PART THREE

THE WONDER OF THE EAGLE IN THE AIR!

HOW TO OVERCOME SINFUL HABITS — ILLUSTRATED FROM THE WORLD OF THE EAGLE

- Do You Know How to Wait on the Lord?

- Five Reasons Why We Fail to Overcome Sinful Habits

- Learn the Secret of Victory over Habits—Understanding the Mystery of Being in Christ

- Seven Steps to Conquer Sinful Habits

- Checklist for Victory over Sinful Habits

- Does It Work?

- Further Insights on Overcoming Sinful Habits

- How Temptations Can Turn into Benefits

"*. . . They that wait[1] upon the Lord . . .
shall mount up with wings as eagles. . . .*"

Isaiah 40:31

1. Wait: Hebrew *"qâvâh"*
*To bind together [with Christ's death, burial, and resurrection]; To
intertwine [God's truth of Romans 6, 7, and 8 with our mind, will,
and emotions]; To expect [that temptation will come, and to be ready
to quote Romans 6 and 8 when temptation does come].*

DO YOU KNOW HOW TO WAIT UPON THE LORD?

- Waiting upon the Lord is not a passive attitude—it is a dyamic responsiveness.
- Waiting upon the Lord is living in the reality that, as Christians, we died and rose with Christ.
- Waiting upon the Lord is continually speaking God's truth within our hearts.
- Waiting upon the Lord is quoting God's answers the instant that we are tempted.

WHAT WILL HAPPEN WHEN WE WAIT UPON THE LORD?

When we quote Scripture in order to resist Satan's temptations, we can be compared to an eagle stretching out its wings in a storm. The air rushing over the wings creates the lifting power which is stronger than the force of gravity that would otherwise cause the eagle to fall to the ground. Similarly, reaching out to quote Scripture during temptation helps us to rise above the power of Satan's temptations.

QUESTIONS:

Have you ever prayed for God to give you victory over sin? Yes ☐ No ☐

Do you know why such a prayer is unscriptural? Yes ☐ No ☐

To illustrate the futility of this prayer, think of the times when you have been defeated even while praying for victory.

ANSWER:

God does not want us to pray for victory. He wants us to enter into the victory which Christ has already won by His sinless life, death, and resurrection. In order for us to have victory over sin apart from Christ, we would have to duplicate what He did to achieve it. This is, of course, humanly impossible. Therefore, when a temptation comes, we should immediately pray:

> *Heavenly Father, I thank You that when I became a Christian, I became united with Christ. Now I am a part of all He did, including His victory over sin.*

FIVE REASONS WHY WE FAIL TO OVERCOME SINFUL HABITS:

1. We try to conquer habits in the energy of the soul.

God wants us to exercise spiritual power over habits. Satan wants us to fight habits with the energy of our souls. Our souls (Greek: *psuchē*) consist of our mental power, our will power, and our emotional power. These are no match for the bondage of sinful habits. Only by spiritual power can we conquer sinful habits.

> *"For if ye live after the flesh, ye shall die: but if ye **through the Spirit** do mortify [conquer] the deeds of the body, ye shall live"* (Romans 8:13).

2. We are double-minded.

A double-minded person has a desire to overcome sinful habits and a conflicting desire to enjoy them. God warns that such a person cannot hope for any consistent victory over sin. A double-minded (Greek: *dipsuchŏs*—double soul) person has not yet learned to hate evil; he will be unstable in all of his ways. (See James 1:8.)

3. We fail to understand what it means to be in Christ.

The only way to consistently overcome sinful habits is to enter into the victory which Christ has already won over them. The precise steps for gaining this victory are explained on the following pages.

4. We make provision for sinful pleasures.

We give outward evidence of hating evil when we remove from our lives all provisions for evil. This means cleansing the galleries of our minds of evil imaginations and cleansing our homes of all sensual possessions.

5. We attempt to hide secret sins.

One of Satan's biggest lies is that secret sins will remain hidden. God makes it very clear: *". . . Be sure your sin will find you out"* (Numbers 32:23). The shame and humbling which come when sins are properly confessed are actually a part of God's provision to receive grace and to conquer sinful habits. *". . . God resisteth the proud, but giveth grace unto the humble"* (James 4:6). (See also I Peter 4.)

LEARN THE SECRET OF VICTORY OVER HABITS

Understanding the mystery of being in Christ:

Many Christians fail to have victory over sinful habits because they do not understand what actually takes place when they are born again by the Spirit of God. The following prayer for understanding is based on Ephesians 1:17–23:

Heavenly Father, I pray that You will give me spiritual wisdom and insight to know more about Christ. I pray for that inner illumination of Your Spirit, so that I might realize how great are the riches of Christ and how tremendous is that power which has been available to me since I first believed.

UNDERSTAND WHAT IT MEANS TO BE IN CHRIST BY FIRST LEARNING WHAT IT MEANS TO BE IN ADAM

As medical researchers continue to study the human cell structure with its DNA ladders, they only confirm the incredible accuracy of God's Word. Scripture tells us that each of us was literally a part of Adam.

Because we are a part of the human cell structure of Adam, we are also a part of his sin. This is why the consequences of that sin are a part of our present life. (See Romans 5:12.)

Not only do we experience the consequences of our forefathers' sins, we also experience the benefits of what our forefathers achieved. God explains this concept in Hebrews 7:10 when He gives Levi credit for paying tithes to Melchisedec. In reality, Levi was not even born when those tithes were paid. They were paid by his great-grandfather, Abraham, hundreds of years earlier. Yet God affirmed that Levi had had a part in paying them because he was "in the loins of Abraham" when Abraham paid the tithes.

AT THE TIME OF OUR SALVATION WE BECOME A PART OF CHRIST'S SPIRITUAL BODY AND EVERYTHING THAT HE DID

When we are born again by the Spirit of God, we become members of the Body of Christ. We are then participants in His death, burial, resurrection, and present seating at the right hand of God the Father. This is a spiritual fact which, when understood and believed, will open up a new level of victory over sinful habits.

EXERCISE THE HEARING OF FAITH

Have you ever pictured Jesus dying on the cross for your sin? If you will visualize this truth and then accept Christ as your Savior from sin, you will become a child of God and you will receive eternal salvation.

Have you ever pictured yourself dying *with* Christ on the cross? Visualizing and believing this truth will give you daily victory over sinful habits. *"Knowing this, that our old man is crucified with him, that the body of sin might be destroyed, that henceforth we should not serve sin"* (Romans 6:6).

SEVEN STEPS TO CONQUER SINFUL HABITS

As branches are engrafted into a wild apple tree . . .

. . . Scripture can be engrafted into our mind, will, and emotions.

1. Engraft Romans 6 and 8 into your soul.

Sinful habits are stronger than the power of the mind, will, and emotions to overcome them. However, by engrafting God's truth into our souls and by living through the power of God's Spirit, we will have the ability to conquer every sinful habit. *"For sin shall not have dominion over you: for ye are not under the law, but under grace" (Romans 6:14).*

Engrafting Romans 6 and 8 is achieved when these chapters of Scripture become a living part of our daily thoughts, will, and emotions, and when we spontaneously quote them the instant that we are tempted.

By engrafting different varieties of good apple branches into the trunk of a wild apple tree, we will be able to enjoy good apples from those branches. In the same way, if we engraft the truths of Romans 6 and 8 into our souls, we will enjoy the good fruit of those chapters. Their fruit is the power to overcome sin and live by the strength of God's Holy Spirit.

". . . Receive with meekness the engrafted word, which is able to save your souls" (James 1:21).

2. Meditate on these verses day and night.

Meditation is turning Romans 6 and 8 into a personal prayer and quoting it to the Lord as we go to sleep at night, as we get up in the morning, and whenever we are tempted throughout the day. (See Deuteronomy 6:7.) Thus, Romans 6:1–3 would be turned into the following prayer:

> *What shall **I** say then? Shall **I** continue in sin, that grace may abound to **me**? God forbid! How shall **I**, being dead to sin, live any longer therein? Don't **I** know that when **I** was baptized into Jesus Christ **I** was baptized into His death?*

The more that we meditate on this Scripture, the more it will become a living experience in our daily lives.

Meditation is both the means of engrafting Scripture into our souls and the by-product of that engrafting.

Meditation is a pleasant "murmuring" of Scripture to ourselves. (See Psalm 1:2.) It is a quiet reflection on the words of Scripture. (See Psalm 119:99.) It is communing with God in the language of His own Word. (See Psalm 119:48.)

Meditation involves repeating the same Scripture over and over, but each time emphasizing a different word and trying to visualize it. By picturing the words, we will be able to turn Romans 6:1–2 into the following prayer:

> *What shall I say then? Shall I continue in this sinful habit of _____, that grace may abound to me? God forbid! How shall I, being dead to this sinful habit of_____, live any longer therein?*

3. Picture yourself dead to the power and appeal of sin.

God tells us that, as Christians, we are dead to sin. (See Romans 6:2.) Our death took place with Christ's death. (See Romans 6:6; Galatians 2:20; and Colossians 3:3.) God wants us to live in the reality of this truth; Satan, however, wants us to believe that we are still slaves to sinful habits.

Initially, Satan seems to have the advantage, because a dead man is not responsive to temptation; and we are often very responsive to temptation. This will change, however, if we trust God's Word rather than our human reasoning.

God told Abraham and Sarah that they would have a son, but Abraham was almost one hundred years old, and Sarah was almost ninety years old. She had been barren all of her life, and it appeared to be humanly impossible for her to conceive. But Abraham believed God's Word in the face of human impossibility. His belief was counted to him for righteousness, and God's Word came true in his life.

Similarly, God tells us that we are dead to the power and appeal of sin. This seems humanly impossible; yet if we believe it and affirm this truth in our hearts, it will be counted to us for righteousness and will come true in our lives.

The process of meditation is comparable to the rumination of a cow. She chews her cud, swallows it, and later brings it up to chew some more.

"For he that is dead is freed from sin" (Romans 6:7).

If we tell ourselves a lie long enough, we will eventually believe it and act upon it. If this is true for a lie, how much more should it work for the truth.

For this reason we are to continuously speak the truth in our hearts. (See Psalm 15:2; Romans 12:2; and Psalm 1:2.)

4. Make no provision for sinful habits.

When we make provision for sensual pleasure, we give Satan the advantage he needs to keep us in bondage to sinful habits. It is for this reason that God commands us over and over again to put away all evil influences from our lives.

"Wherefore seeing we also are compassed about with so great a cloud of witnesses, let us lay aside every weight, and the sin which doth so easily beset us, and let us run with patience the race that is set before us" (Hebrews 12:1).

"Flee also youthful lusts: but follow righteousness, faith, charity, peace, with them that call on the Lord out of a pure heart" (II Timothy 2:22).

"Be not deceived: evil communications corrupt good manners" (I Corinthians 15:33).

"But I say unto you, That whosoever looketh on a woman to lust after her hath committed adultery with her already in his heart" (Matthew 5:28).

"Love not the world, neither the things that are in the world. If any man love the world, the love of the Father is not in him. For all that is in the world, the lust of the flesh, and the lust of the eyes, and the pride of life, is not of the Father, but is of the world" (I John 2:15–16).

"Wine is a mocker, strong drink is raging: and whosoever is deceived thereby is not wise" (Proverbs 20:1).

"The graven images of their gods shall ye burn with fire: thou shalt not desire the silver or gold that is on them, nor take it unto thee, lest thou be snared therein: for it is an abomination to the Lord thy God. Neither shalt thou bring an abomination into thine house, lest thou be a cursed thing like it: but thou shalt utterly detest it, and thou shalt utterly abhor it; for it is a cursed thing" (Deuteronomy 7:25–26).

"But put ye on the Lord Jesus Christ, and make not provision for the flesh, to fulfil the lusts thereof" (Romans 13:14).

5. Compare the law of sin to the law of gravity.

The pull of a sinful habit can be enormously strong. It can make its victim feel just as helpless as a person falling through the air.

A sinful habit is simply the evidence of the law of sin, which continues to affect our lives. This law of sin involves forces within us which we know are wrong.

> *"I find then a law, that, when I would do good, evil is present with me. For I delight in the law of God after the inward man: But I see another law in my members, warring against the law of my mind, and bringing me into captivity to the law of sin which is in my members. O wretched man that I am! who shall deliver me from the body of this death?" (Romans 7:21–24).*

The law of sin in the spiritual world can be compared to the law of gravity in the physical world.

The law of gravity involves forces which have predictable results. The law of gravity is universal: the same results will take place anywhere in the world. Every creature is subject to its effects, whether it wants to be or not.

If an eagle which is soaring in the air suddenly draws in its wings, the law of gravity will take over and that eagle will plunge to its destruction.

It will not take very long for that eagle to fall to the ground. However, if the eagle were to stretch out its wings while falling, the air rushing over its wings would create the lift necessary to overcome the law of gravity. It does not annihilate the law of gravity; it overcomes it.

This is precisely what God promises will happen in our spiritual lives if we "stretch out our wings of meditation" and quote Romans 6 and 8 the moment we experience temptation. No matter how strong the temptation, it will be overcome as we speak God's truth in our hearts.

There are several points to remember in order to experience the law of God's Spirit lifting us above the law of sin:

- Purpose to begin quoting Romans 6 at the moment of temptation.
- Visualize the truths of Romans 6, not the sin that we are being tempted to commit.

"There is therefore now no condemnation to them which are in Christ Jesus, who walk not after the flesh, but after the Spirit. For the law of the Spirit of life in Christ Jesus hath made me free from the law of sin and death" (Romans 8:1–2).

- Continue quoting Romans 6 and 8 until the temptation loses its power and appeal.
- Realize that failure to meditate will result in spiritual bondage with serious consequences.
- Remember that victory has already been won by Christ. We are a part of that victory, because we died with Him and rose from the dead with Him.
- *"For he that is dead is freed from sin"* (Romans 6:7).

6. Become accountable to your God-given authorities.

God commands us to be accountable to one another and to exhort one another in order to overcome the deceptions of Satan. One of Satan's lies is that we can sin secretly and no one will ever know about it, or, if we are discovered, there will be no real consequences. But God's Word is very clear:

> *"For there is nothing covered, that shall not be revealed; neither hid, that shall not be known. Therefore whatsoever ye have spoken in darkness shall be heard in the light; and that which ye have spoken in the ear in closets shall be proclaimed upon the housetops"* (Luke 12:2–3).

• *Use the power of shame to conquer temptation.*

If you knew that all of your secret thoughts and actions would be flashed on a screen for all to see, would it make a difference in your life?

The public shame of sin helps us to comprehend the fear of the Lord. Only by the fear of the Lord do men depart from evil. The fear of the Lord is the constant awareness that God is watching and weighing every thought, word, action, and motive.

• *Establish the right accountability with the right people.*

Ask those who are responsible for your spiritual welfare if they would periodically check up on you. Encourage them to ask you the following questions:

> *What Scripture did you meditate on as you went to sleep last night?*

Are you continuing to live in victory over sinful habits?
When was the last time you experienced spiritual defeat?

Accountability should always be discreet, yet clear enough to let your authorities know of the victories or defeats which you are experiencing.

7. Recognize and obey the Scriptural promptings of God's Spirit.

Conquering sinful habits requires that we reckon (or consider) ourselves dead to sin; but we must also reckon ourselves alive to God. In our battle against sin, we are not to be overcome with evil, but we are to take the offensive and overcome evil with good. (See Romans 12:21.)

Every day, God gives Scriptural promptings to His children. To the degree that we obey these promptings in the power of His Spirit, we will experience success in the Christian life.

What types of promptings does God's Spirit give us?

The Spirit of God may prompt us to:

- Give a word of encouragement to someone
- Pray for each person whom God brings to mind
- Talk to someone about salvation
- Give a particular amount of money according to Scriptural direction
- Remain silent in a certain situation

How are we to respond to God's promptings?

God instructs us to obey the promptings of His Spirit in the very same way that we used to obey the sensual prompting of sin. "*. . . For as ye have yielded your members servants to uncleanness and to iniquity unto iniquity;* **even so now yield your members servants** *to righteousness unto holiness*" *(Romans 6:19).*

HOW WE YIELDED TO SIN

1. We experienced a sensual desire (e.g., to look at a sensual picture or television program).
2. We visualized the sensual pleasure that we would receive from this act.
3. We made the decision to fulfill our sensual desire.
4. We became the servant of sin. *"Know ye not, that to whom ye yield yourselves servants to obey, his servants ye are . . ."* (Romans 6:16).
5. We yielded the members of our body to carry out the sensual pleasure (our hands to pick up the pornographic material or to turn on the television, our eyes to look at the lewd material, our minds to imagine further evil).

HOW WE NOW YIELD TO GOD

1. We experience a Scriptural prompting (e.g., to invite someone for a meal, or to acknowledge when we are wrong).
2. We visualize the action required to obey this prompting.
3. We make a decision to obey the prompting.
4. Our decision confirms that we are God's servant.
5. We yield the members of our body to carry out God's prompting (e.g., we use our mouth to invite someone for a meal, our hands to prepare it). (See Romans 12:1–2.)

CHECKLIST FOR VICTORY OVER SINFUL HABITS

All of the seven steps to conquer sinful habits are essential in order to achieve continuous victory.

It will be very easy to neglect one of these steps. However, if this occurs, Satan will gain an advantage.

For this reason the following checklist is very important.

1. I have memorized Romans 6 and 8:1–15.
   - ☐ I have asked others to quiz me on this Scripture.
   - ☐ I can quote this Scripture perfectly.

2. I am meditating on this Scripture day and night.
   - ☐ I can personalize Romans 6 and 8.
   - ☐ I have purposed to put myself to sleep each night while quoting Scripture.

3. I picture myself dead to the power and appeal of sin.
   - ☐ When I am tempted, I visualize how a dead man would respond to sin.
   - ☐ While quoting Romans 6, I name the sin that I am tempted to commit.

4. I have removed every provision for sinful habits.
   - ☐ I have cleansed my mind of impure imaginations.
   - ☐ I have cleansed my home of sinful objects.

5. I compare the law of sin with the law of gravity.
   - ☐ When tempted, I picture myself falling to destruction.
   - ☐ I instantly quote Romans 6 and picture the principles of aerodynamics taking over.

6. I am accountable to God-given authority.
   - ☐ I have told my parents about the temptations I face.
   - ☐ I have asked them to check up on my daily victory.

7. I am obeying the promptings of God's Spirit.
   - ☐ I fast to increase my alertness to God's promptings.
   - ☐ I have presented my body as a living sacrifice to God and my members as weapons of righteousness for His daily use.

DOES IT WORK?

One who conquered moral impurity

"Before becoming a Christian, I was consistently defeated by a particular sinful habit. I tried to break it many times. I would struggle against it for a short while, but then it would overpower me.

"After I became a Christian, I experienced new power to overcome this habit, but its pull was still there. Soon it enslaved me again.

"Then I learned how to overcome sin by claiming Christ's victory over it. I spent over a month memorizing Romans 6. Then I meditated on it daily. I pictured the truth that I died with Christ and rose with Him. Now, as long as I speak this truth in my heart, I can rise above the law of sin like an eagle soaring above the law of gravity.

"The results have been amazing! I have had continuous victory over this habit. Whenever I am tempted, I immediately quote the truths of Romans chapter six. In a matter of moments the temptation disappears like a mist on a sunny morning.

"Never have I felt such freedom. I can ride over the enemy because Christ crushed his head on the cross. I am dead to sin. I am free!"

One who conquered anger and hatred

". . . One day my hate for my immature tyrant of a foreman grew worse than it had ever been. That very evening I found a Seminar supplement in my mailbox. It had a picture of an eagle on the cover. I was too frustrated to think of anything but hate, so I just set it on the kitchen table.

"The next two days at work were just as bad. Finally, when I got home, I forced myself to read that booklet. As I read, I couldn't believe what was happening to me! It seemed like it was talking to me personally—explaining just what was happening to me at the shop.

"The next day the foreman and I started to lock horns again, but I remembered something from that booklet: *Shall I continue in anger that grace may abound? God forbid! How shall I, being dead to anger, live any longer therein?*

"As I claimed those words for myself, my anger turned into quiet words and a pleasant smile. Through Christ, a potential battle was turned into a pleasant conversation!

"Three times that day there were situations which produced festering hate. Each incident was followed by a Christ-like response. My heart soared as I left the shop that afternoon to come right home and reread that booklet, only to be lifted higher when I read the part about the eagle soaring in the air.

"The truths I learned have taught me how to let my new nature in Christ become stronger than my old nature in the world."

FURTHER INSIGHTS ON OVERCOMING SINFUL HABITS

Illustrated from the world of the eagle

• The eagle was created to fly in the heights of the sky, not to live on the level of the ground.

• The eagle's wings are designed to soar in the air continually. The Christian was made to speak God's truth in his heart continually. (See Psalm 1:2–3; Romans 12:2; I Thessalonians 5:17.)

• If a soaring eagle pulls in its wings, the law of gravity will take over, and the eagle will fall to the ground. If a victorious Christian stops meditating on the truth of God's Word, the law of sin will take over, defeating the Christian.

• A falling eagle needs only to stretch out its wings, and the air rushing over those wings will lift it up again. A Christian facing temptation needs only to quote Romans 6 and 8 and obey the promptings of God's Spirit; and the law of the spirit of life in Christ will lift him up above the law of sin and death. (See Romans 8:1–2.)

• The eagle's very life depends upon its ability to fly above the dangers of the earth. The Christian's ability to overcome the power of sinful habits depends upon his desire to reckon himself dead to sin and alive to God. (See Romans 6:11.)

"But they that wait upon the Lord
[by quoting God's truth of our victory in Christ]
shall renew their strength;
they shall mount up with wings as eagles;
they shall run, and not be weary;
and they shall walk, and not faint."

Isaiah 40:31

HOW TEMPTATIONS CAN TURN INTO BENEFITS

Temptations are like turbulent winds. Responded to wrongly, they can destroy our lives. Responded to Scripturally, they can strengthen our lives.

1. **Turbulent winds cause the eagle to fly *higher*.**

   There is tremendous lifting power in the thermal updrafts of turbulent winds. These updrafts cause the eagle to reach great heights as he soars with them.

2. **Turbulent winds give the eagle a *larger* view.**

   The higher the eagle flies, the larger will be his perspective of the land below him. From this higher position, the sharp eyes of the eagle are able to see much more.

3. **Turbulent winds lift the eagle *above* harassment.**

   At lower elevations the eagle is often harassed by suspicious crows, disgruntled hawks, and other smaller birds. As the eagle soars higher, he leaves behind all these distractions.

4. **Turbulent winds allow the eagle to use *less* effort.**

   The wings of the eagle are designed for gliding in the winds. The feather structure prevents stalling, reduces the turbulence, and produces a relatively smooth ride with minimum effort—even in rough winds.

5. **Turbulent winds allow the eagle to stay up *longer*.**

   The eagle uses winds to soar and glide for long periods of time. In the winds, the eagle first glides in long shallow circles downward and then spirals upward with a thermal updraft.

6. **Turbulent winds help the eagle to fly *faster*.**

   Normally, the eagle flies at a speed of about 50 miles per hour. However, when he glides in wind currents, speeds of well over 100 miles per hour are not uncommon.

*The power of the Christian to rise
above pressures and temptations comes from
identifying with the death, burial,
and resurrection of Christ:* "That I may know him,
and the power of his resurrection, and
the fellowship of his sufferings, being made
conformable unto his death."
Philippians 3:10

HOW THE MESSAGE OF THIS BOOK
HAS BEEN APPLIED

"I have been engrafting Romans 6 and it worked! The Lord helped me to lose eighty pounds in the last year."

Young Lady

"The handles for dealing with sinful habits helped me to stop a habit of eighteen years. What a joy to have this new freedom!"

Pastor

"For many years I have been struggling with moral impurity. Although I read several books on having victory over sin, I just couldn't put it all together. When I realized that my power to rise above pressures and temptations comes from my identification with the death, burial, and resurrection of Christ, I finally experienced victory over sin."

Serviceman

"After engrafting Romans 6 into my life, I have a joy in my heart that is inexpressible! I have been freed of the bonds of rock music and here are just a few of the results: an immediate reduction in the amount of temptation I received, a new light on Scripture—as if my mind was clearer, and no desire to ever listen to rock music again.

"Last night I took all of my rock tapes (even though I had not listened to them in a year) and burned them. What a refreshing freedom to know that they are out of the house!"

Teen-ager

"Although I knew Romans 6–8 for years and even taught it to others, I lived all my life in moral defeat. I got involved in homosexuality and no one was aware of my plight. Then I heard of the principles of Christ's death, burial, and resurrection, and the Lord opened my eyes to the way of victory. Now I have complete freedom from the chains of sin."

Teacher

"I was so encouraged to learn about overcoming sinful habits. I memorized Romans 6 and then meditated on these verses at least twice a day all year. However, I still was not free of my sin. You see, the shame that my sin produced kept me from confessing the problem to one in authority over me. Finally, in desperation I decided deliverance was more important to me than my remaining dignity, and I confessed my sin. Now I have freedom from sin in this area and even freedom from its desire."

Christian Worker

"For half of my life I have struggled with a lust problem that I just could not conquer. I engrafted Romans 6 into my mind and it worked fairly well; but then I fell back into sin. Some key was missing and I couldn't put my finger on it. Later, through a tragic experience, something profound happened to me—I learned the meaning of the word 'humility.' Now that I have combined humility with Romans 6, I've found that it really does work!"

Young Man